What Do Animals Do On the Weekend?

—Adventures from A to Z—

Written and Illustrated by

Lauren Faulkenberry

NOVELLO Festival PRESS

For Tyler—
with the hopes
that all of
your weekends
are filled with
adventure—
Lauren
1/21/05

Book Design by Leslie B. Rindoks

Library of Congress Cataloging-in-Publication Data

Faulkenberry, Lauren, 1978-
What do animals do on the weekend? : adventures from A to Z /
written and illustrated by Lauren Faulkenberry.
p. cm.
Summary: Recounts the leisure time activities of a variety of creatures,
from ants admiring paintings in an art gallery to zebras looking at New
Zealand from their zeppelin.
ISBN 0-9708972-4-3 (hardcover)
[1. Animals--Fiction. 2. Recreation--Fiction. 3. Alphabet.] I. Title.
PZ7.F2688 Wh 2002
[E]--dc21
2002000147

NOVELLO FESTIVAL PRESS, CHARLOTTE, NC.
First Printing

For Mom and Dad
—L.F.

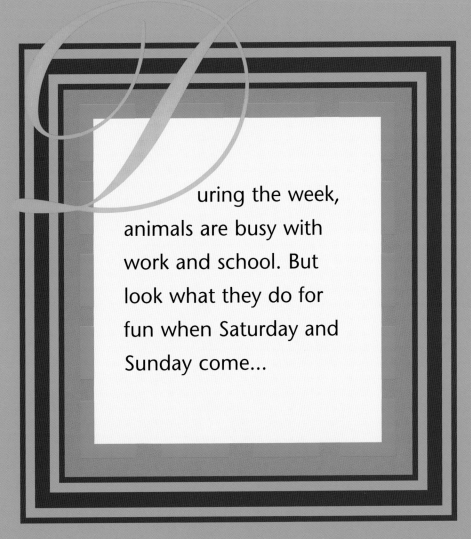

uring the week,
animals are busy with
work and school. But
look what they do for
fun when Saturday and
Sunday come...

 **A**nts in an art gallery?

Absolutely! All afternoon, Andy

and Anita admire the amazing

array of paintings.

An array is an important or large display of people or things.

elinda Bobcat and her

brother, Boris, play in a band.

Boris keeps the beat on the bass

while Belinda sings the blues.

Tonight, Bartleby Bear joins in

with his bugle.

The string bass is six feet tall, making it the largest instrument played

with a bow. Blues is a style of music that can sometimes be sad.

rocodiles are crazy

about the cha-cha. Charlie and

Corinna could dance all night at

the coolest club in the city.

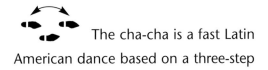 The cha-cha is a fast Latin American dance based on a three-step  rhythm. A saltwater crocodile can grow to be 20 feet long!

**D**essert at the downtown diner is simply divine. David Dachshund and his daughter Darla drop by every weekend to split a double-dip milkshake.

Dachshunds, the national dogs of Germany, were once trained to chase  badgers. Diners are restaurants that sometimes look like train cars.

xploring at the equator? Emus really enjoy that. This evening in Ecuador, Elizabeth and Eric come out early to see the eclipse.

A lunar eclipse occurs when the earth's shadow is cast on the moon.

The equator is an imaginary line dividing the earth into two halves.

Fiji is a fun place for foxes. Frank and Felicia go fishing each fall when the islands are twinkling with fireflies.

 DID YOU KNOW? Fireflies are found on every continent except

Antarctica. Fiji is a nation of more than 800 islands in the Pacific Ocean.

Goodness gracious!
These goats are golf pros. Grace
and George play the greens every
weekend, but Grace gets grumpy
when a goose grabs the ball.

The first club for golfers was begun
in Scotland in 1744, although there are
written records of people golfing as
long ago as 1457.

arvey and Heidi Husky

are happy to stay at home and

play hide-and-seek in the house.

Harvey isn't hard to find, but

Heidi can vanish like Houdini.

The Siberian husky is an arctic sled dog. Harry Houdini was a magician who was  famous for escaping from jail cells, handcuffs, and tanks of water.

ce skating, what a great idea! Ian and Irene Impala decide to hit the ice, since it's much too nice to stay inside.

If you were an African impala, you could leap 30 feet at a time!

IMAGINE THIS: People were skating on ice more than 2,000 years ago!

ackals just love to jitterbug. Jake and Julie go out every week to jump and jive to their favorite songs on the jukebox.

The jitterbug is a fast dance that was first popular in the 1940s. A jukebox is  a coin-operated machine that plays music from records or discs.

**K**angaroos get their

kicks when they kayak in Kenya.

Kevin keeps paddling across the

lake while Kyra plays her kazoo.

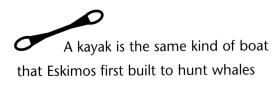 A kayak is the same kind of boat that Eskimos first built to hunt whales

thousands of years ago. Kenya is a country in eastern Africa.

 ouis and Lana

Leopard like to dance the

lambada at a local Latin club.

They linger until late, not

wanting to leave.

The lambada is a graceful ballroom
dance from Brazil. Leopards are good

climbers and sometimes
eat their dinners up in the trees.

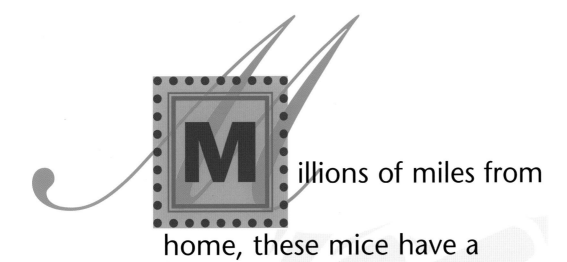

Millions of miles from home, these mice have a marvelous view. Marvin and Macy chase comets and moonbeams on their mission bound for Mars.

Mars is called the red planet because of its rusty-colored soil. Though it can be seen from Earth, it's never closer than 34 million miles away.

othing could be nicer than sailing at night. Nate and Nora Newt use the stars as their guide as they navigate north down the Nile.

The Nile flows north through Africa, and is the longest river in the world.

Sailors once used the brightest stars to navigate, or find their way.

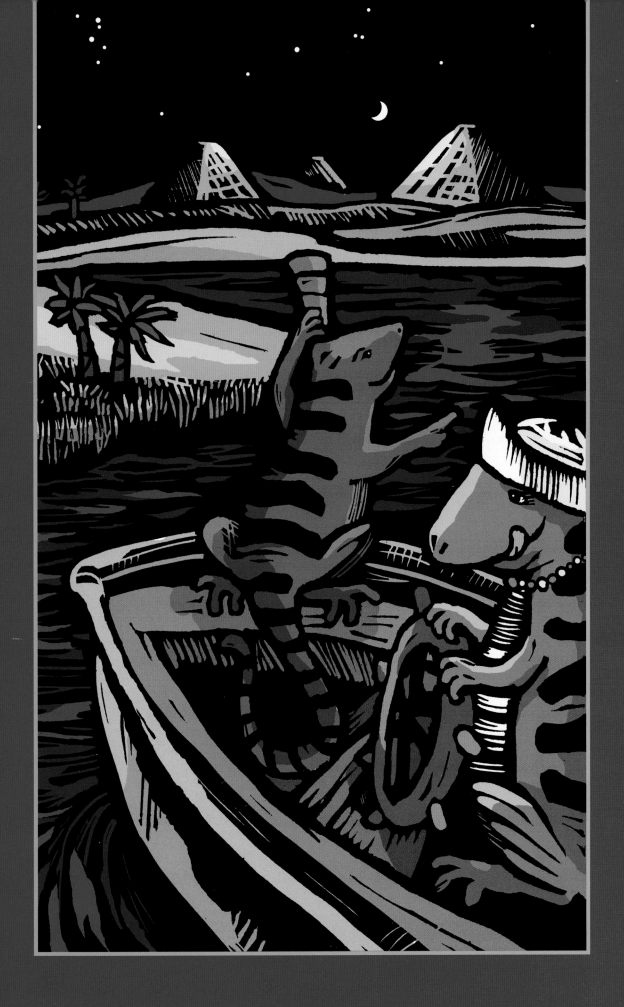

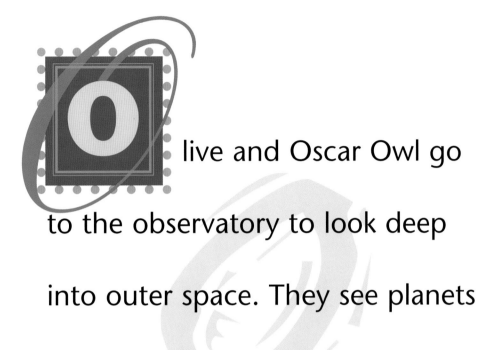

Olive and Oscar Owl go

to the observatory to look deep

into outer space. They see planets

in orbit, oodles of stars, and their

favorite constellation, Orion.

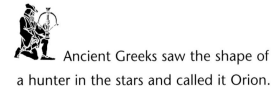
Ancient Greeks saw the shape of a hunter in the stars and called it Orion.

An orbit is the curved path of a planet or moon through space.

enguins love a good picnic, so Pierre and Paula pack a lunch. Peaches, plums and pleasant weather make for a perfect day in the park.

There are no penguins at the North Pole — they live only in the southern  hemisphere. Emperor penguins can grow to be 4 feet tall.

 uentin and Queenie Quail

have quite a talented family. When

Quinn and Quincy sing on key, they're

the hottest quartet in Quebec — no

question or quarrel about it.

A quartet is a group of four singers or musicians. Quebec is an eastern province of Canada where most people speak French.

iding along in their

roadster, Ralph and Rita

Rhinoceros take a road trip to

Reno. Rita turns the radio up,

and Ralph rolls the top down.

 Route 66 is a famous highway
that goes from Chicago to Los

Angeles — that's more than 2,400
miles! A roadster is a kind of sports car.

 **S**heep say the sea is the best place to be in the summer.

Sam surfs the waves on sunny days, and his sister Sylvie cruises in her sailboat.

Can you believe people were surfing in Hawaii before Christopher Columbus sailed for America in 1492? Cowabunga!

Time after time, Tabitha and Toby Tiger go out for a night on the town. It takes two to tango, and this team could dance until twelve.

In Argentina, they dance the tango. Tigers, the largest members of the cat family, can weigh 450 pounds. (That's the same as 50 house cats!)

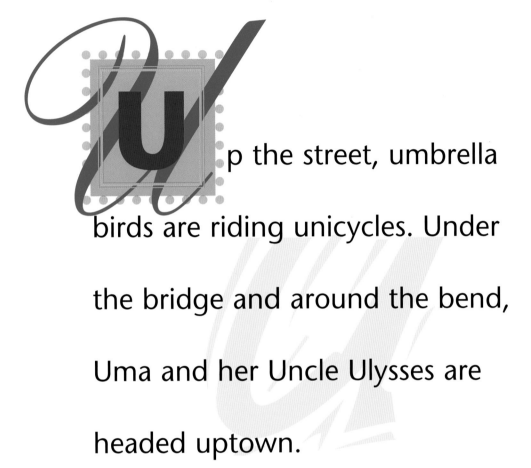

Up the street, umbrella birds are riding unicycles. Under the bridge and around the bend, Uma and her Uncle Ulysses are headed uptown.

Umbrella birds live in the treetops of rainforests in South America.

You need very good balance to ride a unicycle — it has only one wheel.

enice is a beautiful vacation spot for vipers. Veronica loves to drift through the vast canals while Vincent plays his violin for her.

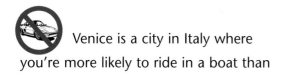 Venice is a city in Italy where you're more likely to ride in a boat than  in a car. It has more canals filled with water than streets!

**W**here do wombats go on weekends? Walter and Wendy walk through the woods when the weather is nice and warm.

Australia is full of unusual animals such as kangaroos, koalas and wombats.

Wombats build homes in the ground, and dig while lying on their sides.

ander and Xena

Xenops are excellent musicians.

These rainforest birds get their

exercise playing exotic tunes at

Club Xanadu.

Xenops are birds that live in South American rainforests. They hang upside  down to eat! Xanadu was a place where royalty lived in China.

Yodel-eh-he-hoo! Yes, it's true — these yaks like to yodel. Yvonne and Yuri go to the Yukon each year for a camping trip full of surprises.

 The Yukon, in western Canada, is so far north the temperature has reached

81 degrees *below* zero! Yodeling, a style of singing, is very popular in Switzerland.

**Z**ooming through the air in their zeppelin, Zack and Zoe Zebra zig-zag through the clouds until the sun sets on another zany weekend.

A zeppelin is like a hot air balloon, but it's shaped like a football.

Zebras are from Africa, and no two have the same pattern of stripes.

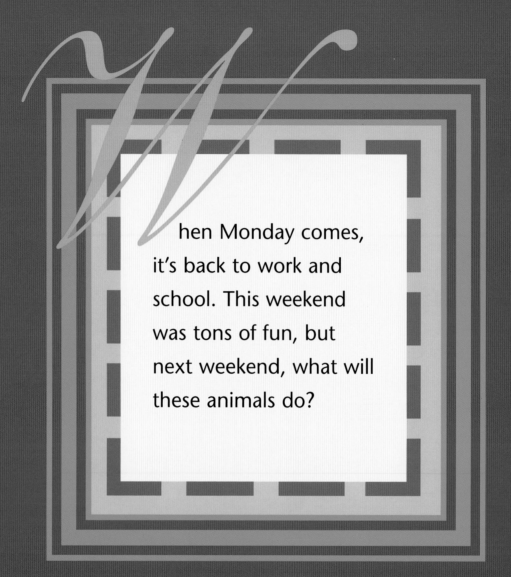

When Monday comes, it's back to work and school. This weekend was tons of fun, but next weekend, what will these animals do?

Can you find something else in each picture beginning with that letter?

(If you need a hint, look at the alphabet inside the covers.)

About the Author

Lauren Faulkenberry grew up in Kershaw, South Carolina, and currently works as a freelance illustrator, writer and mural painter. She earned her B.F.A. at Washington University in St. Louis, where she began watching all sorts of animals on the weekends.

She has always had a passion for books, and it was in art school that she was introduced to the printing press. It was love at first sight. From there she traded in her paintbrushes and went on to study printmaking and handmade book production. The concept for this book was developed based on her love of woodcuts, interest in unusual animal behavior, and preoccupation with the alphabet. The illustrations are linoleum block prints, colored digitally.

No animals were harmed in the making of this book!

Acknowledgments

The author wishes to thank her family and friends for all of their love and support, and especially Stephanie, who lived amongst piles of inky linoleum blocks and never once complained about the smell. She also wishes to thank every teacher she ever had, from her kindergarten teacher to her thesis director; World Book Encyclopedia, Microsoft Encarta, the Illustrated Oxford Dictionary, EnchantedLearning.com, and Professor James E. Lloyd, for his expert knowledge of fireflies.

She offers special thanks to everyone at the Public Library of Charlotte and Mecklenburg County, Novello Festival Press, and especially to Amy and Frye, for making her dream a reality.

Novello Festival Press

Novello Festival Press, under the auspices of the Public Library of Charlotte and Mecklenburg County and through the publication of books of literary excellence, enhances the awareness of the literary arts, helps discover and nurture new literary talent, celebrates the rich diversity of the human experience, and expands the opportunities for writers and readers from within our community and its surrounding geographic region.

The Public Library of Charlotte and Mecklenburg County

For more than a century, the Public Library of Charlotte and Mecklenburg County has provided essential community service and outreach to the citizens of the Charlotte area. Today, it is one of the premier libraries in the country — named "Library of the Year" and "Library of the Future" in the 1990s — with 23 branches, 1.6 million volumes, 20,000 videos and DVDs, 9,000 maps and 8,000 compact discs. The Library also sponsors a number of community-based programs, from the award-winning Novello Festival of Reading, a celebration that accentuates the fun of reading and learning, to branch programs for young people and adults.

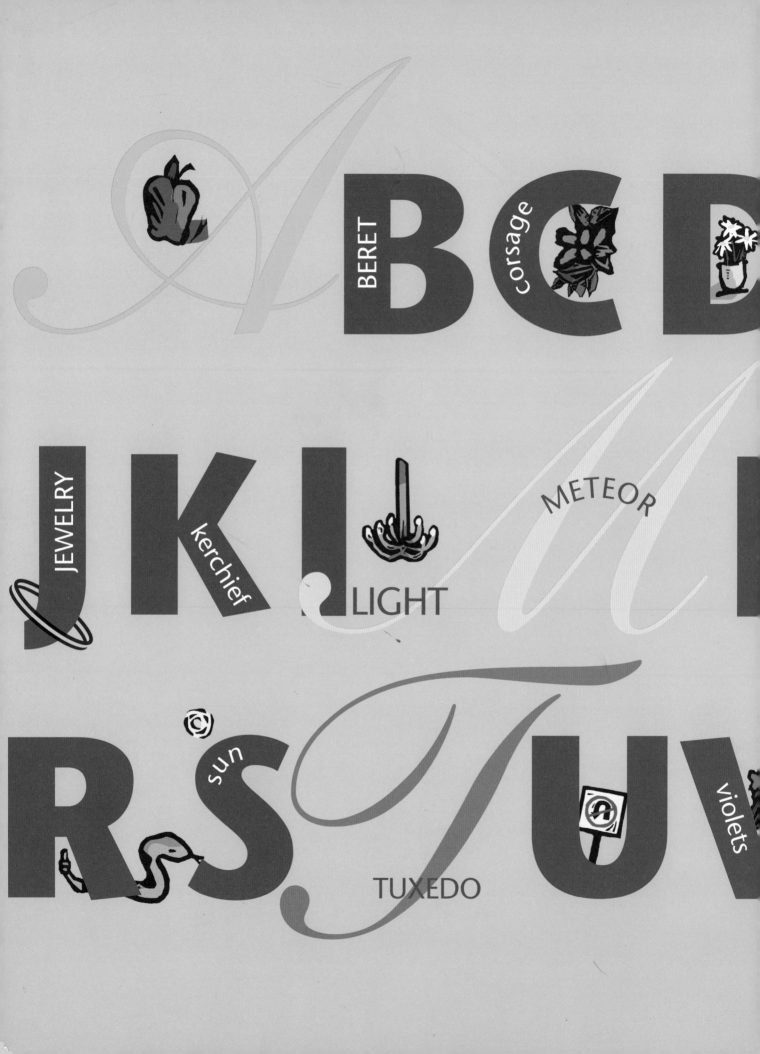